On the Tail Trail

Dalmatian Press, 2008. All rights reserved. Printed in the U.S.A. 1-866-418-2572
The DALMATIAN PRESS name and logo are trademarks of Dalmatian Press, LLC, Franklin, Tennessee 37067.
No part of this book may be reproduced or copied in any form without written permission from the copyright owner.

08 09 10 11   B&M 33343 10 9 8 7 6 5 4 3 2 1
17524 Disney My Friends Tigger & Pooh 8x8 - On the Tail Trail

"Abracadabra!" said Darby.

"Hooray!" cheered Roo. "We just love your magic show, Darby!"

"Oh, oh, my!" said Piglet. "However did you do that?"

"Most mystifying," added Tigger.

Darby giggled. "And now for my next trick," she announced, "I will make a ball roll right across this table!"

"Well, that's not so amazing," muttered Eeyore.

"And I'll make it stop and then roll in a circle," said Darby.

"Oh, oh, my!" said Piglet.

"Watch this!" Darby declared.

She placed a small ball on the table. She waved her magic wand—and the ball began to roll! Then it stopped! Then it rolled again—in a circle!

"I don't suppose," said Pooh, "that a little breeze is making
that little ball move… just a little?"

"Nope!" said Darby.

"Oh, oh, oh, my!" said Piglet, trembling.

Darby smiled at Piglet. "I'll show you how I did it," she said.
"But first I need a volunteer from the audience."

"Will a tigger do?" asked Tigger.

"Tigger-rific!" said Darby. "Here—take this…"

"Got it!" said Tigger.

"…and hold it right next to Eeyore's tail."

"Hey—I didn't volunteer, ya know," mumbled Eeyore.

CLICK!

Eeyore's tail came right off—and stuck!

"Hoo-hoo-hoo!" said Tigger. "Magic!"

"It's not magic," said Darby. "It's magnets! The tack in Eeyore's tail came right out and stuck to this magnet."

"Magnet?" said Roo.

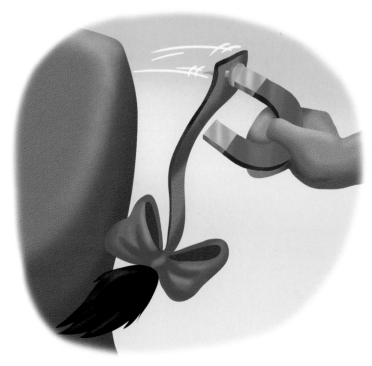

"Yep!" said Darby. "A magnet is made of a metal that does something amazing. It makes some other metal objects—made of iron or tin—come right to it. Look! The red ball has iron inside it, just like Eeyore's tail tack. So when I move the magnet under the table—"

"—the ball moves with it!" cried Piglet. "Oh, oh, my!"

"Fun, fun, fun!" said Tigger. "Will you show us some more magic tricks tomorrow, Dar-Dar? Please, please, and re-please?"

"Sure!" said Darby. "I'll meet you right here in the morning."

But the next morning, as Darby was setting up for her show—

SSuuuUUppppperrrr ssllllEEEUUtthhs!

—the Sleuther Siren was sounded.

Tigger and Pooh and Darby and Buster gathered at the Changing Tree. There was a mystery to be solved!

"Time to slap my cap!" said Darby. "Let's see what the Finder Flag shows us."

"It's Eeyore," said Pooh.
"Lookin' a bit gloomy," said Tigger.
"Come on, Super Sleuths!" said Darby.
"Let's go see what the mystery is."

"Any time, any place,
The Super Sleuths are on the case!"

The Super Sleuths found Eeyore outside his house.
"You look down in the frumps, Eeyore," said Tigger.
"But we're here to help," said Pooh.
"What's the problem?" asked Darby.

"Lost my tail," said Eeyore. "Looked in my house. Looked outside my house. Can't find it."

"Oh, dear," said Pooh. "And you're sorta attached to your tail."

"Not at the moment I'm not," said Eeyore glumly.

"Cheer up, ol' pal," said Tigger. "We Super Sleuths are good at solveratin' mysteries. We'll be on the tail trail in a jiffy."

The Super Sleuths searched all around Eeyore's yard, but there was no trace of Eeyore's tail.

"Okay, team," said Darby. "It's time to think, think, think! Where else could Eeyore's tail be?"

"I don't know," said Pooh. "It's always with Eeyore."

"Exceptin' when it's on the end of a magnet—hoo-hoo!" announced Tigger.

"No need to bring that up at a time like this," muttered Eeyore.

"Hey—that's it!" cried Darby. "Magnet! We could use a magnet to find Eeyore's tail!"

"That's a good idea," said Pooh. "But... er... how?"

"The tack in Eeyore's tail will stick to a magnet," explained Darby. "We can walk around with my big magnet—and that tack will come right to it!"

Soon the Super Sleuths and their friends were on the trail of that tail. Darby's big magnet did find a whistle and a metal button—but no tack—and no tail.

"Oh, bother," said Pooh. "I'm afraid we'll need more magnets."

"Move side! Move aside!" called Rabbit.

"What kind of thing-a-ma-jiggy is that?" asked Tigger.

"It's my super-duper Tack Attractor," announced Rabbit.

"Tacky tractor?" said Tigger.

Rabbit glared. "TACK ATTRACTOR," he sniffed. "I happen to know that magnets *attract*—that's the right word to use. My invention will attract that tack!"

Rabbit attached Darby's magnet to the end of his contraption. Then he and the Tack Attractor went all over the Hundred-Acre Wood with the magnet swinging back and forth.

"Still looks kinda tacky to me," whispered Tigger.

Rabbit did find one of
his lost gardening tools.

And he did find a tin pail.
"My drum! My drum!"
cheered Roo.

But no tack—and no tail.

But then, as Rabbit approached Darby's magic-show stage—
something moved in the grass.

"I found it!" proclaimed Rabbit. "There's Eeyore's tail!
It's with some of Darby's magic-show props."

But as he swung the magnet close to the tail…

...the tail moved away!

"Well, now," pondered Rabbit,
"let me try that again."

He swung the magnet close again—and again the tail moved away!

The Super Sleuths gathered around to watch Eeyore's tail dart away from the big magnet.

"Hmmm…" said Tigger. "Eeyore, ol' buddy, it appears that your swisher-oo is doin' the ol' scooter-oo."

"No matter," said Eeyore. "Most likely doesn't want to come back. I will miss it, though."

"We can solve this mystery, Eeyore," assured Darby. "Tigger, take a closer look at Eeyore's tail. Do you see any clues?"

"I see a doozy of a clue!" said Tigger. "That tail tack has gone and gotten itself stuck to one of your magnets."

"That magnet—has—has—made your tail come alive!" said Piglet.

"Tsk-tsk. Ahem!"

Everyone turned and looked at Rabbit.

"Magnets," declared Rabbit, "are quite magical! They can *attract* objects—as I have already told you. But when two magnets get together, they can push each other away—which would explain why that magnet on Eeyore's tail tack was scooting, as you say, away from the big magnet."

"Eeyore, you must have sat down near my props," said Darby, "and your tail came out when it got stuck—"

"*Attracted!*" Rabbit corrected.

"—got *attracted* to one of my smaller magnets."

"Well, thanks, guys," said Eeyore. "Your tacky tractor worked, Rabbit. Didn't expect it to. But I'm kinda glad. It's not much of a tail…

...but I *am* sorta attached to it."